Piero and Roberto after the war.
Rome, 1945.

Sabina holding Roberto.
Rome, 1939.

Roberto, Sabina, and Piero. USA, 1948.

P9-CBR-806

THESE PHOTOS ARE OF MY FAMILY: My mother, Sabina; her first husband, Jacob; and their children, Roberto and Piero (whom I've changed into young Nonna). This is their story. —Marisabina Russo

Sabina and Jacob (in white trousers). Italy, 1934.

Roberto, Sabina,
and Piero.
Mountains of Italy, 1944.

In memory of my mamma, Sabina, and my brothers, Piero and Roberto

GLOSSARY

Anti-Semitism – Discrimination against Jews because of their religious beliefs and ethnic background.

Cara mia – My dear.

Concentration camps – Harsh prison camps created by the Nazis. Millions of Jews were deported to these camps, along with other ethnic and political groups. Most prisoners were killed or died because of the terrible conditions.

"Fa la nana, bambin" – Italian lullabies are known as *ninne nanne*. There are many variations. *"Fa la nana, bambin"* can be translated as "Rock-a-bye, baby."

Grazie a tutti – Thank you all.

Internment camps, enforced residence – Two types of detainment of Jews used by the Italian government. Internment camps were more like prisons, while enforced residence allowed people to live in private homes in villages with less supervision.

Nazis – The followers of Germany's leader, Adolf Hitler. The name is derived from Hitler's political party, the National Socialists.

Nonna – Grandmother.

Partigiani – Partisans, resistance fighters who planned and carried out secret attacks on the enemy.

Piazza – City or town square.

Polenta – A dish made from ground cornmeal or chestnuts. It is similar to grits.

Ragazzi – Children.

Signor and *Signora* – Mr. and Mrs.

Zabaglione – A custard-like dessert made with egg yolks, sugar and wine.

Copyright © 2011 by Marisabina Russo. All rights reserved. Published in the United States by Schwartz & Wade Books, an imprint of Random House Children's Books, a division of Random House, Inc., New York. • Schwartz & Wade Books and the colophon are trademarks of Random House, Inc.

Visit us on the Web! www.randomhouse.com/kids
Educators and librarians, for a variety of teaching tools, visit us at www.randomhouse.com/teachers

Library of Congress Cataloging-in-Publication Data
Russo, Marisabina. I will come back for you : a family in hiding during World War II / Marisabina Russo.
p. cm.
Summary: A grandmother tells her granddaughter the story of the charm bracelet that represents her own childhood experiences while she and her family tried to evade the Nazis in Italy during World War II.
ISBN 978-0-375-86695-1 (trade) — ISBN 978-0-375-96695-8 (glb) — ISBN 978-0-375-98515-7 (ebook)
[1. Grandmothers—Fiction. 2. Bracelets—Fiction. 3. Jews—Italy—Fiction.
4. World War, 1939–1945—Italy—Fiction. 5. Italy—History—1914–1945—Fiction.] I. Title.
PZ7.R9192Iam 2011 • [E]—dc22 • 2010044523

The text of this book is set in Archetype. • The illustrations were painted in Winsor & Newton gouache on Arches 140-lb cold-press watercolor paper.
Book design by Rachael Cole
MANUFACTURED IN CHINA • 10 9 8 7 6 5 4 3 2 1 • First Edition

Random House Children's Books supports the First Amendment and celebrates the right to read.

I WILL COME BACK FOR YOU

A FAMILY IN HIDING DURING WORLD WAR II

MARISABINA RUSSO

schwartz & wade books · new york

My Nonna changes her jewelry every day, but there is one bracelet she always wears. It is a charm bracelet, a gift from my mama.

Sometimes we sit together and Nonna lets me touch the tiny charms— a donkey, a piano, a bicycle, a piglet, a barn, a spinning wheel, and a boat.

One day I ask Nonna why she never takes off her bracelet.

"Because the charms remind me of long ago when I was a little girl," she says. "Shall I tell you their story?"

"Yes, Nonna!" I answer right away.

And so she begins.

"When I was smaller than you, I lived in an apartment with tall windows that looked out over a busy piazza in Rome."

"In Italy," I say.

"Yes," says Nonna.

"Every afternoon my mamma took your great-uncle Roberto and me to a park called the Villa Borghese. They had puppet shows and a caffè for ice cream and even donkey rides." Nonna touches the donkey charm. "I loved those rides, but Roberto, he was sometimes frightened. He thought the donkeys might gallop too fast."

"Did they?" I ask.

"Oh no," says Nonna. "They were very gentle. Afterwards Roberto and I would chase each other up and down and all around the paths. Occasionally we would see soldiers. Roberto liked to salute them.

fa la nana, bel bambin . . .

"Late in the afternoon when we were tired and cranky, Mamma walked us home. After dinner we had our baths, put on our pajamas and waited for Papà. Every evening he played the piano for us before we went to bed."

I rest my head on Nonna's shoulder as she softly sings a song I've never heard before—
"'*Fa la nana, bambin, Fa la nana, bel bambin . . .*'

"It was a happy time."

"But then things started to change for us—for all the Jews in Italy. New laws said Jews were not allowed to own radios or go to certain beaches or even attend public school. One day the police chief of Rome ordered Papà to leave our family and move to a small village up in the mountains."

"Why?" I ask. "Did he break one of the new laws?"

"No," says Nonna. "A terrible war had broken out in Europe. When Italy joined the German side, the government started rounding up foreign Jewish men like Papà, who was from Poland. The Nazi government in Germany had been treating Jews unjustly and now Italy was, too."

Nonna looks away. "All I knew was that I missed my papà. Our apartment was too quiet without his laughter and his music."

Nonna touches the tiny piano charm on her bracelet.

"On the weekends Mamma would take us on the train to the mountains. I remember the very first time. We arrived at the station and so many donkeys were lined up in a row. Roberto started to cry."

"Scared of the donkeys!" I say.

"Exactly," says Nonna. "Luckily, Papà was waiting for us, and Roberto jumped into his arms. We rode in a wagon to the village where a family— the Silvestris—let us stay with them. They had a yard full of chickens and their own donkey, too. Poor Roberto. Donkeys everywhere!

"The hardest part was that Papà was not allowed to stay overnight with us. He had to sleep at the inn where he lived with all the other Jewish men who were being detained. It wasn't really a jail, they could come and go as they liked, but every morning they had to report to the police station for roll call.

"During the day we had lots of fun with Papà. We played marbles and had running races and he sang to us before our naps. But every Sunday evening we had to say goodbye and return to Rome.

"And we had no idea our separation would last months and then years.

"One weekend Papà came to Mamma with some terrible news. I was outside feeding the chickens, but I could hear them talking through the window. Papà said he'd learned that the Germans were coming to the village. They planned to send all the Jewish detainees to a concentration camp, a real prison in Germany. Papà was going to run away and hide.

"'Don't go, Papà!' I called, jumping up and down in front of the window. "'*Cara mia*, I must leave,' Papà replied. He leaned out and lifted me into his arms. Then he whispered, 'I will hide a message for you and Mamma in the trunk of the old beech tree at the bend in the road so you will know I'm safe. Then you must go back to Rome. When the war is over, I will return.'

"Papà made me promise not to tell Roberto about the plan. He didn't want my little brother to give everything away.

"That same evening Papà slipped away with only the clothes he was wearing. The next morning a policeman came looking for him because he'd missed roll call. Mamma just shook her head and said, 'I have no idea where he is.' The policeman grew angry and replied, 'Well, Signora, since we must deliver seventeen Jews to the Germans tomorrow, we will send you instead. Pack your things. I will be back this evening to collect you.'

"Roberto and I were very scared. When Mamma put us to bed, she said, '*Bambini*, do not worry. I will never let them take me away.' But what could my mother do?

"That evening I sang to Roberto, *'Fa la nana, bel bambin . . . ,'* until we both fell asleep. We didn't know that Signora Silvestri and her two brave sons, Carlo and Rodolfo, had a plan.

"Carlo made a terrible concoction of hot water and cigar leaves and told Mamma to drink it. It would give her a fever and make her dizzy, and if she was too sick to travel, the transport would have to leave without her. Oh, how sick she became after only a few sips!

"When the policeman returned, Mamma was curled up in bed. Still, he said, 'No matter. The transport is not until tomorrow. I will sit in front of the house in case you try to escape.'

"Carlo and Rodolfo carried their most comfortable chair outside for the policeman. They brought him a big plate of spaghetti and two bottles of wine. And guess what? Before long, he was snoring away."

Nonna shows me her tiny bicycle charm. It has
wheels that really spin.

"Now the two brothers roused Mamma," she
says. "They carried her out the back door and made
her sit on the handlebars of Carlo's bicycle. Holding
Mamma with one arm, Carlo pedaled farther up into
the mountains, to an old farmhouse. The farmer, a
friend of the Silvestris, was a kind man who did not
like the war. He helped poor sick Mamma into his
barn, where she fell asleep on a bed of hay.

"I was so scared when I woke up and Mamma was gone. And there was such a commotion outside. The policeman was yelling at Signora Silvestri. Carlo and Rodolfo were yelling back. Roberto kept crying, '*Dov'è Mamma?* Where's Mamma?'

"As we watched from the doorway I whispered, 'Don't worry. She will come back for us.'

"Finally, when the policeman was gone, Signora Silvestri hugged us. '*Ragazzi,* you are safe with me until your mamma can return,' she said. 'For now you will be my children.'

"But we didn't *want* to be her children. Roberto and I both cried every day, even though Signora Silvestri made us delicious foods like polenta and zabaglione, and her sons kicked soccer balls with us.

"Roberto followed me everywhere, afraid that I would disappear, too. *How could Mamma just leave us?* I kept wondering.

"A few weeks later a neighbor, Signor Brunelli, stopped by, leading a donkey with baskets strapped to its back." Nonna pauses to touch the little donkey charm on her bracelet. "'Would you like to go for a ride, *bambini*?' he asked. 'Yes, yes!' I said, but Roberto started to cry. Signora Silvestri whispered a secret. 'Signor Brunelli is going to take you to your mamma.'

"Signor Brunelli helped us into the baskets. What a surprise! There were piglets in each one! Signora Silvestri had us crouch down. Then she placed a small cloth on each of our heads and on top of that . . . a piglet."

"Like little piglet hats!" I say.

"True," says Nonna with a smile, touching the piglet charm on her bracelet. "Everyone in the village knew that Signor Brunelli took his piglets higher into the mountains to trade with other farmers. Who would suspect that huddled under the baby pigs were two small children?

"It was a long, bumpy ride. I listened for Roberto, but if he was crying it was drowned out by the piglets' squealing."

"They must have missed their mamas, too," I say.

"Yes!" says Nonna. "Then at last we reached the farmhouse, but we didn't see Mamma anywhere. The farmer's wife led us to a field where women in long skirts and head scarves were working. One rushed over and covered us with kisses. It was Mamma!"

Nonna smiles and shows me another charm. It is a barn with a tiny door that opens and closes.

"That night Mamma told us she'd found Papà's note in the trunk of the beech tree. He was hiding farther up the mountains. When it was safe we would all be together again.

"For many months we stayed at the farm. We played with the farmer's children, and Mamma worked in the fields. She learned how to carry water jugs on her head and even how to spin yarn from sheep's wool. We all looked like part of the farmer's family, so no one suspected we were Jews."

I touch the spinning wheel charm.

Now Nonna has a faraway look. I wait for her to finish the story.

"And what about your papà?" I finally ask.

"We never saw Papà again," says Nonna. "Later we learned that he'd joined the *partigiani*, a group of people who were fighting against the Germans. It was very dangerous. One day a couple of Nazi soldiers found his hideout. They killed him."

Nonna gently runs a finger across all the charms of her bracelet. "At last, on a beautiful day in June, the war was finally over in the mountains. Mamma took Roberto and me back to Rome. But the city was in such chaos! Strangers were living in our apartment, there were long lines for food, there were few jobs.

"Mamma decided it was time for us to leave, and so we sailed for America.

That is why I have this charm." Nonna shows me a tiny ocean liner.

Now one by one I touch the charms. When I get to the donkey I say, "Thank you for helping my Nonna."

"Yes, *grazie a tutti*; thank you to the donkeys, the piglets, the brave Silvestris, the kind farmers," Nonna says. Then she kisses my forehead. "Isn't that a long story for such a simple charm bracelet?"

"No," I say. "It's exactly right."

I Will Come Back for You is based on a story I often heard as a little girl. It is all true—the detainment; the visits; and the cigar drink, bicycle escape, and piglets—but I have changed the ending for the sake of simplicity.

In 1933, because of growing anti-Semitism, my mother, Sabina, and her first husband, Jacob, left Nazi Germany to settle in Italy. For several years they lived peacefully, as Jacob set up a medical practice and Sabina gave birth to two sons. They loved their adopted country.

Unfortunately, a few years later Italy also began passing laws discriminating against Jews. However, unlike Germany, Italy did not—at first—imprison them.

World War II began in 1939 after the Nazi invasion of Poland caused France and Great Britain—known as the Allies—to declare war on Germany. On June 10, 1940, Benito Mussolini, Italy's dictator, declared Italy's entrance into World War II on the side of the Germans. The very next day, Italian police began to round up foreign Jewish men like Jacob, sending them first to prisons and then to internment camps or enforced residences. Women and children later joined the men. Sabina managed to avoid this fate because of a friendship with a minister in the government who gave her papers allowing her and her sons to remain in Rome. They visited Jacob on weekends.

In late 1941 the United States entered the war on the side of the Allies. The Italian armies suffered great losses, and in September 1943 Italy surrendered to the Allies. But this did not bring an end to the fighting. The German army, already scattered throughout Italy, was determined to push back the Allies. Some of the fiercest battles of the war occurred in Italy after it had surrendered.

Life became much more dangerous as the German army swept through, trying to crush opposition and deport the remaining Jews. Despite the risk, many Italians chose to hide their Jewish neighbors. Incredibly, about eighty-five percent of the Jews in Italy survived the war, more than in almost any other European country.

Bands of men and women formed groups—called *partigiani*, or partisans—to resist the German invaders. They met in secret and blew up bridges, helped wounded Allied soldiers, and did whatever they could to disrupt the German army.

Sadly, Jacob, who joined the partisans, was captured and killed by the Germans in May 1944. Sabina, by then also a partisan, was shot but survived, thanks to nurses who hid her in a hospital laundry room and cared for her. While the Marche region near Rome, where these events took place, was liberated in June 1944, the Germans were not completely defeated in Italy until April 1945.

My mother and my two half brothers came to the United States in 1946. Jacob was posthumously awarded the King's Commendation for Brave Conduct, and my mother was honored with the King's Medal for Courage in the Cause of Freedom, both from the British government. In 1996 she received the title of Cavaliere Ufficiale, one of Italy's highest decorations for public service.

Roberto, Sabina, and Piero after the war.
Rome, 1945.

Sabina and Piero near
their apartment in Piazza
Barberini. Rome, 1938.

Roberto, Sabina,
and Piero at a caffè.
Rome, 1941.

Piero and Sabina.
Rome, 1939.

Roberto and Piero
with a soldier.
Rome, 1940.

For anyone who sat alone on the school bus

IMPRINT
A part of Macmillan Publishing Group, LLC
120 Broadway, New York, NY 10271

ABOUT THIS BOOK
The art for this book is digital painting. The text was set in Burbank Small, and the display type was hand-lettered. The book was edited by John Morgan and designed by Carolyn Bull. The production was supervised by Raymond Ernesto Colón, and the production editor was Dawn Ryan.

Library of Congress Control Number: 2019949523
ISBN 978-1-250-22977-9 (hardcover)

Our books may be purchased in bulk for promotional, educational, or business use. Please contact your local bookseller or the Macmillan Corporate and Premium Sales Department at (800) 221-7945 ext. 5442 or by email at MacmillanSpecialMarkets@macmillan.com.

Imprint logo designed by Amanda Spielman

First edition, 2020

1 3 5 7 9 10 8 6 4 2

mackids.com

Steal this book?
Feeling loot-y?
A curse on you!
This be pirate's booty!

IT'S NOT A SCHOOL BUS, IT'S A PIRATE SHIP

Written by Mickey Rapkin

Illustrated by Teresa Martinez

[Imprint]
MAKE YOUR MARK
New York

"Ready for school, tiger?
Here comes the bus."

"Don't be scared. You're the Master of Mornings.
The Captain of Cool!"

Me, cool? But who will I sit with?
What if nobody talks to me?

"You don't have to be afraid," the bus driver whispered. "This isn't a school bus, it's a

PIRATE SHIP!

SUN!

And flying fish! And . . .

a dolphin eating a taco?!

"Ahoy, matey! My name's Zenzi!
Wanna hear a joke?
What's a pirate's favorite letter of
the alphabet?"

Why was I so scared?
We're all in the
same boat!

SCHOOL BUS

"Follow me!" Zenzi said.
"It's all hands on deck
for a scallywag sing-a-long!"

Yo ho, yo ho! A quiet ride for me?

No ho, no ho! A pirate riot, weeee!

"Hey, now *I've* got a joke.
What's a pirate's favorite vitamin?"

"Rough seas ahead!" the captain shouted.
"Buckle up, buccaneers!"

Is the ship gonna stink? I mean SINK?

"We've got this," Zenzi whispered.
"Pirates are one for all. And all for FUN!"

Could it be . . . ? Dry land, ho!

"Good morning," the teacher said.
"Find a spot on the rug!"

"It's not a rug," I whispered to Zenzi.
"It's a magic carpet!"